THIS BOOK
BELONGS TO:

Sweet Dreams

Copyright © 2023 by Rick Telander

All rights reserved. No part of this book may be reproduced in any manner without the express written consent of the publisher, except in the case of brief excerpts in critical reviews or articles. All inquiries should be addressed to Skyhorse Publishing, 307 West 36th Street, 11th Floor, New York, NY 10018.

Skyhorse Publishing books may be purchased in bulk at special discounts for sales promotion, corporate gifts, fund-raising, or educational purposes. Special editions can also be created to specifications. For details, contact the Special Sales Department, Skyhorse Publishing, 307 West 36th Street, 11th Floor, New York, NY 10018 or info@skyhorsepublishing.com.

Skyhorse® and Skyhorse Publishing® are registered trademarks of Skyhorse Publishing, Inc.®, a Delaware corporation.

Visit our website at www.skyhorsepublishing.com.

10 9 8 7 6 5 4 3 2 1

Library of Congress Cataloging-in-Publication Data is available on file.

Cover design by Brandtner Design Ltd.
Cover art by Rick Telander

ISBN: 978-1-5107-7833-7
Ebook ISBN: 978-1-5107-7835-1

Manufactured in China, May 2023
This product conforms to CPSIA 2008

Sweet Dreams

Poems and Paintings for the Child Abed

RICK TELANDER

and His Artist Friends

DESIGN BY BRANDTNER DESIGN LTD.

Skyhorse Publishing

The Child Abed

I was once a little boy
So very long ago.
My sisters, they were little girls,
And then we all did grow.

But never once have I forgot
My cozy childhood bed,
The comfort, prayers, and fevers, too,
The poems I was read.

For nighttime comes, it always does,
And sleep and dreaming, too.
Our bedtime offers peace and hope,
The skies a starry blue.

So let this be my humble gift,
This book of verse and joy,
A handing down from me to you,
Each sleepy girl and boy.

Rick Telander

Dream

If my bed were a boat,
I would want it to float
Down a quiet gold stream
Deep inside of a dream.

If my boat were a bed,
I would lay down my head
On a pillow as sweet
As a wind-rippled sheet.

If my room were the world,
I would know that it twirled
Around peace in its place
With a smile on my face.

If the world were my room,
There would never be gloom
When I turned off the light
And the day became night.

If it all were a dream,
I would float down that stream
Under heavenly skies
Till I opened my eyes.

illustration by **GREG RAGLAND**

Rising Moon

The moon got stuck in a tree tonight,
A branch to the left
And one to the right.
The bough above held him down that way —
This was not a place
For the moon to stay.

I know that the moon is my good friend,
So I closed my eyes
That I could pretend
That I was as strong as any man —
And the tree became
A twig in my hand.

I bent all those limbs, their price to pay,
For blocking the path
To the Milky Way.
A cloud rolled in, a silvery veil —
And then rolled along
With darkening trail.

My eyes were shut a moment or two,
Or maybe I slept,
No matter if true,
For when I looked out, the moon was free —
Alone in the night,
And he winked at me.

illustration by ANITA KUNZ

Pill

A pill
Is a hill,
Two
Neat ones—
A plateau in between.

The thrill
Is the will
To
Eat one—
Thrice-daily lima bean.

illustration by NANCY DREW

Prism

The sun is yellow,
A one-tone fellow,
But some of his rays
Have colorful ways.
The shaft that comes in
The window at ten
Strikes my glass abed
And then turns to red
And purple and green
And paints a bright sheen
On a wall that's white
In regular light.

At ten there are glints
Of colors and tints
That hide like a dream
In that little beam
Till it stripes the wall
With a pattern small
But wonderfully bright
For colorless light.
The shades must be there,
Like wind in the air,
Like sugar in tea,
Like salt in the sea.

Or else they reside
In the crystal side
Of a water glass
Where little can pass.
But I doubt that's so,
The sun makes things grow,
And I will presume
When it spears my room
At that morning hour
And bursts like a flower
It shows me a part
Of its warming heart.

I wonder each day
While waiting that ray:
Am I like the sun,
Have my hues begun?

Midnight Universe

Today I did nothing.
Nobody noticed me.
I floated like a speck,
Ignored unmercifully.

But tonight's a new tale,
Book, chapter, page, and verse,
When I become the lord
Of the Midnight Universe.

Behold, I am massive,
My muscles engineered!
They call me Grell the Great,
Dragon-Slayer Most Feared.

Sing out, shining broadsword!
Fly, evil and the vile!
Timid stand behind me—
Yon wicked face your trial!

Ever in the distance,
Trolls and fiends plot revenge—
The Great One never sleeps;
In sleep he doth avenge!

illustration by JILL THOMPSON

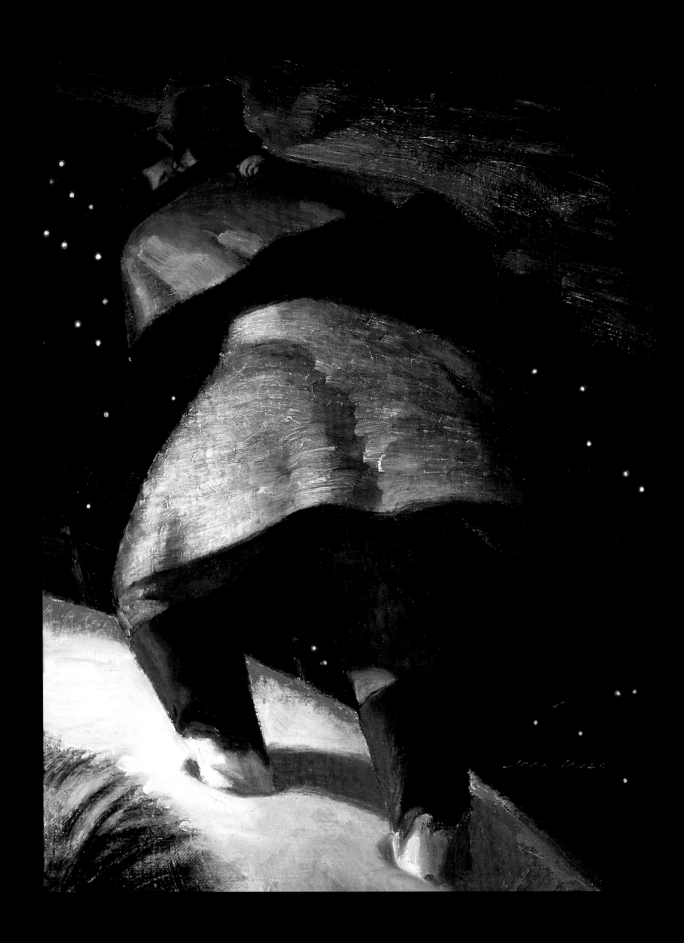

Night Journey

One night my father held me close,
When I was tired and longed to sleep.
He buttoned me into his coat
And walked the path unlit and steep.

He held me to him with an arm;
The cold wind tore the sky apart.
He was proof against the storm,
And I became his beating heart.

Boys of Summer

The baseball game begins at one.
By then I'll have my duties done—
My books all stacked, a clean nightstand,
The bedspread clear, my glove at hand.
Then out I'll bring my wooden box
With Reds and Yankees, Cubs and Sox—
Pretty little paper sluggers,
Hurlers, twirlers, stealers, pluggers—
A card for every man afield,
An All-Star gang with bats to wield.
I'll move them through my park of green,
In mirror of the men ascreen.

I play a game within the game—
I make each throw, I take the blame
For lazy fly balls hit to right—
You never swing with all your might!—
But each home run belongs to me,
Or to my men (my praise is free),
And by the seventh-inning stretch
I'm tired, I yawn, I lean to fetch
My box where soon the boys retire
To grumble, heal and then conspire,
To talk about what might have been,
To sleep and then to play again.

illustration by **BILL WILLIAMS**

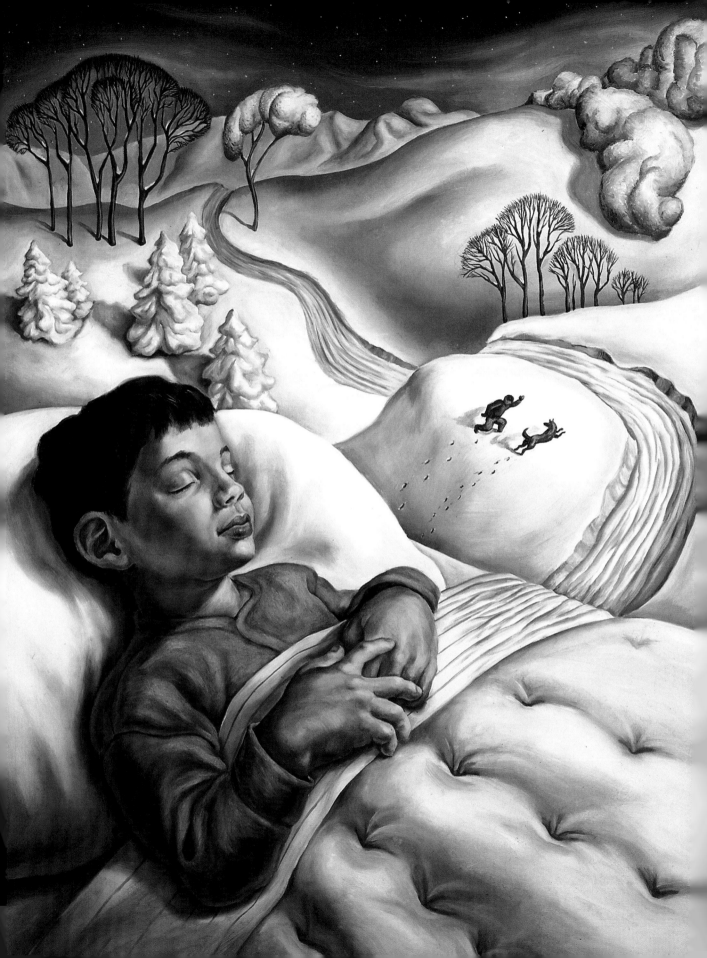

A Snowy Night

The snow falls down like finest fluff
That's pulled from cotton plants and stuff.
The wind's soft hands removed it so
And bore it gently months ago,
From crimson soil of sun and drought,
A present by the Southern route—
Way up and up into the clouds
That veil us yet in deepest shrouds—
And there the cotton mixed so nice
With eiderdown and whitest ice,
All turned and tooled to stars of cold,
Of silver bright and palest gold,
And heavier than air should be,
It now falls down on top of me.

It doesn't; No—I feel it still,
Beyond the glass, beyond the sill,
A cape of hope, a cooling shield,
That girds the lane, the trees, the field.

Bumpy Afternoons

I never can get comfortable,
No matter what I do.
I think I'd rather ride a bull,
Than take a nap at two.

So Snorter ratchet up a notch,
Make this the Wild West —
I feel a thing that's like a watch,
Fast-ticking in my chest.

It tells me I should be up top,
Your horns tight in my hand,
Just like we're in a china shop,
All bullish through the land!

illustration by JIM SWANSON

Solstice
(DECEMBER 21)

The violet sky,
The trees of black,
The ground of white
Reflecting back
The faintest, sweetest,
Softest tune
Of winter peace
Unto the moon.

illustration by JULIAN ALLEN

Morning Glory

Oh, little girl, in the wakening dawn,
Do you see the jewels that sparkle the lawn?
Do you see the glow,
Do you see it grow,
Do you see the colors the angels have drawn?

Oh, little girl, in first morning light,
Did you have a safe and wonderful night?
Did you travel far,
Did you touch a star,
Did you sail the sea of purple and white?

Oh, little girl, what goes through your mind?
Do you see the good in the things that you find?
Do you see the face,
Do you feel the grace,
Do you know the world is gentle and kind?

A Splendid Machine

I made a wheel while lying here,
Then glued it to a little gear.
The gear I carved, to tell the truth,
From balsa and each little tooth
Is not precise — some are not there —
But still it works, revolving fair,
And turns another just like it,
But larger which itself does fit
Into a third hooked to a shaft,
Hooked to a fourth with greatest craft,
And that one turns upon its stand,
And spins a bright blue rubberband,
That turns a rod hooked to a gear,
That twirls a hoop that does appear
To show that engineers, dear me!
As silly as they want to be.

Summer Dusk

Is that Mother calling?
I think I do not hear—
So few ways of stalling,
With bedtime racing near.
Why does the day keep growing
From morning until night?
Adventure overflowing,
With dimming of the light.

I hear steps behind me,
The whippoorwill his song,
The sky a pale ruby—
Why can't the day go on?
"Sleepy-time," comes the voice,
The dreaded grownup tune.
I sit without a choice,
A prisoner of June.

I stamp my foot and glower,
Old Fuzzy at my side.
I sigh and pick a flower—
I'll take the day inside.
And lying in my room
With all the world unfair,
I'll smell my summer bloom
And dream I am out there.

illustration by **MARK SAUCK**

Saturday Night

Up the stairs the music flows,
Then slips beneath my door.
Shouts and laughter rise and splash,
A tiny ocean's roar.

My room is washed in late-night surf,
My ears and mind are stressed.
How can a child expect to sleep
When grownups will not rest?

illustration by **JASON MILLET**

The Hammock

My hammock life
Is sweet indeed—
A leaf falls on me,
Then a seed.

Grandpa used to
Lie just so,
His arms like this
And rocking slow.

He said I'd soon
Appreciate
Autumn's bounty,
Summer's fate.

Appreciate?
What should I do—
Forget my ball?
And playground too?

I laughed back then,
I wouldn't slow.
I was a child
Two years ago.

But now I look
Into the sky
And smile at things
That catch my eye:

Another leaf,
A dozen more—
The bluest blue,
A squirrel's chore.

I hear a call—
Perhaps the birds
That flutter South,
Or Grandpa's words.

The Softest Bed

The animals I like are these:
Eagles, snails and chimpanzees.
I'm also rather fond of hogs
And salamanders under logs.

But most of all I love the fox,
The red one dashing over rocks,
That loses hounds and will descend
Into a safe and cozy den.

And there he curls into a ball,
His tail a quilt to cover all.
How thankful in my bed I'd be
If I could wrap myself in me!

illustration by **NEESA BECKER**

Reputation

What can I draw that lasts forever?
What can I say so very clever,
To which they'll bow,
And tell me how,
They've never known such brilliance, never!

I need to leave my mark today—
A poem, perhaps, or molded clay.
It must be great,
For I am eight—
I will have fame without delay!

The City Game

So sweet the beat of basketballs
When I must go lie down.
I hear it when I wake again,
The cheery, rubber sound.

My friends are there along the court—
They watch the big men play.
Grandma says I need my rest,
And will all through the day.

Whacka-whacka,
In the sun.
Whacka-whacka,
Never done.
Whacka-whacka-whacka.

Being sick in summertime
Is not what I had planned.
I want to put my sneakers on
And join my merry band.

Instead of shorts, I wear my jams,
The ones with polka dots.
I'm separated from my pals,
Connected by my thoughts.

Whacka-whacka,
All day long.
Whacka-whacka,
Summer song.
Whacka-whacka-whacka.

I am a star, and they're stars, too—
I pass the ball and slash.
The ball comes back, I launch myself,
And dunk it with a crash.

I wave to Al, he waves to me,
And Grandma calls my name.
I doze once more, surrounded by
The rhythm of the game.

Whacka-whacka,
Sing to me.
Whacka-whacka,
Symphony.
Whacka-whacka-whacka.

Tiger and Lamb

I am the Tiger burning bright,
Who holds the Lamb with all his might.
So fierce and strong; you see my jaws?
I scorch the earth, I laugh at laws!
But little Lamb I hug in glee,
As God above He cradles me.

illustration by **JEFFREY SMITH**

The Shaman

When the desert sun has slipped to the West,
And the canyons are rearranged blue,
And the stones and spires and trees purple-up,
And the mesas are violet, too —
Then he appears like a shade on the rock,
With the air a faint perfume of sage;
I float through the wide and fabulous sky
To the Shaman alone on his stage.

"Mr. Wolf," I say, "please finish the tale
That you started before the half-moon.
Tell how the desert became what it is
And the rivers all fell into ruin.
Tell how you taught the eagle to see
And the lizard to grow a new tail.
Tell how the cactus was armored with spikes —
And who rides the high-mountain trail."

His wings spread wide as I sit on his knee
And the animals gather around.
Sparkles of stars fall away from his glove,
And his voice is the night's only sound.
He talks of the riddle that wraps the world,
And the magic that binds it as one;
The dog is the cat, he says to us there,
And the moon is the child of the sun.

He tells us of things that surely must be,
Of coyotes who fell from the black;
There are bears on high and jewels in the sand,
And we ride on a great turtle's back.
Who can explain how the mysteries go
In the light of the shimmering day —
But Shaman at night weaves truth out of dark,
Till the sun sends us all on our way.

illustration by LEE MacLEOD

Lucky Ducks

If you see a duck,
It brings good luck.
If you see two,
Much better for you.
If you see three,
Then you will see:
When you see four,
There will be more.

My Hyper Friend

Explain to me the hummingbird—
It rockets in and then—absurd!—
It stops like this and shoves its beak
Into a flower without a squeak.
And zip! it rockets out again,
Straight back, straight up, straight down and then
Another flower, another spear—
A nervous blur from there to here.

The thing about the hummingbird
Is in its head has it occurred
To round its flight and savor it,
To maybe just relax a bit?
Please take a cue from Mr. Hawk
And float the breeze without a squawk—
Hummingbird, I'd feel less queasy
If you once could take it easy!

illustration by **JENNIFER KOURY**

Fever

When down is up and up is down,
And this side's that and square is round,
There is no sense that I can see
That keeps you sitting here by me.
Why does your chair not lose its place
And Teddy Bear float into space?
Why don't the curtains fly about,
Since there is here and in is out?
I'll stroll the ceiling—Here I go!
Over the dome light, smartly so.
Look at the table hanging there,
And my own bed up in the air!
Now down the wall I lightly walk
And back to where we two can talk.
So tell me, in this magic room,
What room is there for care or gloom?

Mother

I hear you reading poems to me
With messages that I can see
Should lift me up above all this,
Beyond the little things I miss.
But I hear no words, just your voice,
And in its melody rejoice.
The words are silent singers of
A deeper music and your love.

illustration by **NICK BUBASH**

Day and Night

The little boy was dreamy tired,
The cat far less than he.
But true, the clock said nine o'clock,
In bed he soon would be.

"Silvie, I'm about to drop.
And you, my furry friend?"
The cat meowed and stretched her paws,
Then shook from tip to end.

Softly, she rose up and stepped
From desk to covered chair.
Her claws she used liked tenterhooks,
Then sprang into the air.

Atop the dresser, quickly down
And over to the bed,
Across the pillows, past the crease
Where soon he'd lay his head.

She stopped just once and looked at him—
"Please follow me." He knew.
She led him to the outside door—
He opened, she was through.

A blur into the darkened woods,
Where she might hunt 'til dawn—
How unalike the two of them,
He thought with sleepy yawn.

Her leaving so reminded him
That no one is the same—
Each one of us feels different things
Called by a different name.

What wakes you up might tire me out,
Your thrill might be my fright—
Some creatures live their best by day,
Some live their best by night.

illustration by **FRANKLIN McMAHON**

Pill Again

I do know this about the pill—
You take it when you're feeling ill.
And if you take it when you're well—
Well, why do that, pray tell?

So here's a friendly tip from me—
Please down your pill most carefully.
Here's to your health and here's to mine—
Mine? Why, I'm nearly fine!

illustration by **KEN CALL**

Seasons

Summer is hot,
Winter is not.
Fall works both ways,
Spring rains for days.

I like them all,
Sun and snowfall,
Drizzle and sleet,
Hailstones and heat.

Why is it so?
How could I know?
Comfort take wing,
Change is the thing.

Questions

Whatever could be the reason
I feel the way I do?
Is it for pulling sister's hair
Or losing my left shoe?

Or did someone find out my scores
Or look under my bed?
I promise I will clean it up—
Or was it what I said?

I really don't hate vegetables—
Surely, that is well known.
I hid the spinach in my cuff,
But that was overblown.

Does some adult not like me so,
Or have I been that bad?
I wouldn't make a child this sick—
Not even just a tad.

Then who could have done this to me?
And Mother does reply,
"It was nobody, there's nothing—
No simple reason why.

"You're good and dear, my little boy.
Don't strain yourself to think.
I'll tidy up your pillows now—
Please have something to drink.

"Then won't you say a little prayer
And dream of something kind?
This too will pass, believe me, son."
Her words so ease my mind.

So, yes, I pray as best I can,
Including friend and foe,
And then I set my sails to where
The summer breezes blow.

illustration by **MOSES X. BALL**

The Garden

When I awoke I was a worm,
And through the muddy world must squirm.
For this role I never asked,
But in the sun had always basked.

Now in the dark I feel my way
Down narrow halls of wetted clay.
Boulders here and there appear,
Still on I dig through paths unclear.

At once I pop into the light—
A sudden birth, uncertain sight.
Joy to be above the ground—
A robin stalks there with no sound!

So quickly back into my hole
I pull, aware of daylight's toll—
Yet a scene remains with me:
A garden fair beneath a tree.

With furrows lovely, dark and deep,
It's to their mysteries I'll creep.
Under footsteps, under all,
Through sightless, muffled night I'll crawl.

I wouldn't choose to be a worm—
I'd rather walk my earthly term,
But having now a worm's soul
A garden has become my goal.

When My Best Friend Stops By

(THE VOWEL POEM)

I pray
Today
You stay
And play,

That we
May see
What we
Can be,

Though I
Am shy,
I try,
Don't I?

And though
You know
I go
Too slow,

Still you,
Me too,
We two
Are true.

Richard Forster

The Rooster

The nights are warm in old Key West,
The trade wind blankets all.
One thing alone disturbs my rest:
The sidewalk rooster's call.

A grander chicken never strode
Nor strutted through the dark,
His harem not quite in the road,
Or nestled in the park.

Each eve his gang will settle in
Beneath McDougal's truck—
Then through the peace there comes a din,
And I am out of luck.

It's not the hens or chicks in fluff
Who shrilly spew the noise.
It's only Mr. I-Am-Tough,
The-Badddest-of-the-Boys!

He thinks he's brave, he's mean, he's cool,
When blaring out his cry.
But what I think is he's a fool
And in a pan should fry.

I'm really not that mad at him,
It's just that I'm so tired,
When stars are out, the moon is dim,
And suddenly he's wired.

The church bell rings, it's three o'clock,
And no way can I sleep
Because this big old howling cock
Won't let me count my sheep.

They say that roosters crow at dawn
To greet the morning sun,
A show of joy and feathered brawn,
To tell us night is done.

It's different, though, in Old Key West—
The sidewalk rooster knows.
He glares at me and puffs his chest
In constant macho shows.

Well, fine, okay—you own the land,
The night and sunshine too.
All I can say to you and band
Is, "Cock-a-Doodle-Doo!"

illustration by RICHARD FORSTER

If You
Are Lost

If you are lost, I'll find you.
Should you stray from the flock,
Or miss the marking rock,
There is no ticking clock,
No door I won't unlock—
If you are lost, I'll find you.

If you are lost, I'll find you.
There's nowhere you can lie,
With bleat or softest cry,
No miles I won't defy,
No clue will pass me by—
If you are lost, I'll find you.

If you are lost, I'll find you.
The tempest I will charm,
My fur shall keep you warm,
Dear lamb, fear no alarm,
I'll keep you from all harm—
If you are lost, I'll find you.

My child, I swear,
My soul declare—
If you are lost, I'll find you.

The Night Bird

Sometimes I hear the Night Bird with her sweet and easy song —
It happens when my eyes have closed and doesn't last for long.

She sings to me her melody and takes me on her flight —
I sing with her; I think I do — or is it just the night?

For when I pause my feathered ride, I see the world below —
I look out over stars and clouds to places that I know.

Oh, there's my town, my house, my bed, my little doggy, Shawn —
And there is me just waking up — My goodness, it is dawn!

illustration by TONY FITZPATRICK

Dinosaur Time

Dinosaurs roam through my room—
They came again last night.
A Spinosaurus swam right by,
A Kryptops gave me fright.

But I am safe within my sheets,
With blankets for my walls.
I meekly peek and watch them strut,
And make their screechy calls.

An Analong ate all the grass
That grows beneath my bed.
A Microraptor flew up high,
Just wanting to be fed.

But down below a fierce T. Rex
Reached up and ate him whole!
It roared with satisfaction then,
A massive, toothy troll.

And yet I couldn't help but laugh—
There was a Stegosaurus,
And she was dancing in the mud
Next to a Brontosaurus.

Which, by the way, another one,
Much taller than my room,
Rose up into the trees outside,
Whose leaves she did consume.

Wulongs came, and Yulongs too,
And swift Velociraptors.
Some had big teeth and some had wings,
And all were great adaptors—

For it's a scene from Pleistocene—
Excuse me, Mesozoic—
These ancient creatures in my room,
In numbers quite heroic.

The names are hard and rather weird—
They come from Greek and Latin,
And none of them roll off the tongue
Like feathers do off satin.

But *tri* means three, and *tops* means face,
And *dino*, that means scary.
Tyrannosaurus, you can guess—
To sweetness it's contrary!

To memorize all of these words
You'd have to be a wizard—
It's silly, anyway, I think,
Since *saur* just means lizard.

So, yes, I get a thrill each night
With awe and shock and smiles—
I marvel at the lot of them,
My gang of old reptiles.

illustration by **PEGGY MACNAMARA**

Down in the Valley

Just over the rise where the river runs through,
There down in the valley where yellow meets blue—

Some day I'll go walking, I know that I will.
And won't you come with me, just over the hill?

We slowly could stroll, and I'll take your hand.
The sun and the clouds, the touch of the land—

With you by my side, we'll see what is there—
I dream it already—the smell of the air,

The warm summer blooms, the wind in the trees,
The soft-running river, as sweet as you please.

Oh, won't you go walking with me there some day?
This won't last forever, I've heard what they say.

I love you, it's true, and it comforts me yet,
For I know you love me, so please don't forget—

Just over the rise, where the river will be,
Oh, sister, come with me to see what we see.

The Middle of the Night

Who is awake at this hour?
Nobody, only I.
That anyone should be astir,
I can't imagine why.
I would be asleep myself,
Were I like the others—
Mother, Father, kitty, too,
Sister, Granny, brothers.

Everyone in every place
Is dozing in their bed,
But I am wide awake now
With visions in my head.

The dark is all around me,
But I am not afraid.
I see things that delight me—
So many friends I've made:
The spider in the corner,
The mouse inside the wall,
The cricket by my window,
The fairy queens and all.

So I will lie here softly
Till people do arise,
Midnight music in my ears
And Magic in my eyes.

illustration by **JEAN KIM**

The Architect

I like to build things up,
And then to tear them down.
The castles I erect
Come crashing to the ground.

Sometimes it is a fort,
Sometimes a steeple tall,
That rises like a pine
Before its mighty fall.

They say wrecking's evil,
With laughter only worse.
I say that destruction's
Construction in reverse.

See You in the Morning

Is there a place I'd rather be than right here in my bed?
Would I prefer the swimming pool and splashing friends instead?
Or would I really like to cruise a sunny centerfield,
And snatch deep baseballs from the sky, my talent unconcealed?
Perhaps I'd want to rove just once within a candy store,
And know that everything was free and would be evermore.
But then again, there is the beach, the waves, the shells, the sun —
And sand where I can build empires to humble Babylon!

But would I rather be somewhere that cannot feel as right,
As how I feel when snuggled in my blankets every night?
My bed is warm and soft and sure, my passageway to Nod —
To wish to be another place would be, I think, quite odd.
I'm happy as can be right here; I cannot hide a smile —
Don't grieve for me, just go, and then come back here in awhile,
For now I'm getting droopy-eyed, quite busy counting sheep,
Precisely where I want be — Goodnight — I am asleep!

illustration by **DOUGLAS KLAUBA**

Guardian Angel

Dear little sister doesn't know
Her guardian angel's there —
Gwen fell asleep amidst my words,
And I brushed back her hair.

She's breathing soft, her face at peace,
Again this quiet night.
She often says she'll never sleep —
I let her think she's right.

For it's my joy to share with her
Tales from this book of rhymes
And watch her eyelids slowly close
In harsh or troubled times.

I well remember being four —
It wasn't long ago —
So many nights when I, too, fussed
Or felt the undertow

Of fearsome things and worries vague,
The kinds all children feel,
Until they learn that they are safe,
And angels can be real.

Within her dreams Gwen just might think
That she is all alone,
But she is not, and never is,
Though it may be unknown

To sleepy children everywhere,
Who never have been told,
That God protects his little ones
With angels brave and bold.

artist unknown

Tree Top Melody

Rock-a-bye baby, the lullaby goes —
The infant rocks gently as summer wind blows.
To be in the tree top with leaves all around
In branches quite sturdy so far off the ground —
Oh, give me the chance to fly like a bird,
To rest nearer heaven, the firm land obscured.
The greens of her bounty, the blue of the sky,
The forest around us —just this tree and I —
To be so protected, to gently be held
By dear Mother Nature, my troubles all quelled —
If this isn't solace, then none does exist —
I'll be that rocked baby —I cannot resist.
So rock me forever and sing me to sleep,
The tree is my cradle; its music I'll keep.

The Land of Goodnight

Roll along now on a blanket of fleece,
Roll on through the cotton above—
Roll, little child, on a quilt made of down,
On the wings of a snow-white dove.

Roll along now to the Land of Goodnight,
Roll over the waves and so free—
Roll, little child, on the back of that dove ,
Roll along to the deep blue sea.

About the Artists (IN ORDER OF APPEARANCE*)

GREG RAGLAND is an instructor at the University of Utah, College of Fine Arts, and a founding member of the Santa Fe College of Design in Santa Fe, New Mexico. (9)

ANITA KUNZ is a Canadian artist whose paintings are held in the permanent collections of the Library of Congress, the Museum of Contemporary Art in Rome, and the National Portrait Gallery in Washington, D.C. (10)

NANCY DREW is a visual artist based in Niles, Michigan. Her paintings on canvas, furniture, and mobiles are displayed in many Midwestern galleries. (13)

MARYA VEECK is a Chicago-based artist, exhibiting at her Roscoe Village gallery, August House. She is the daughter of late baseball visionary, Bill Veeck. (14)

JILL THOMPSON is among the first women to illustrate comic book superheroes. Thompson became the artist of DC Comics "Wonder Woman" series in 1990. She has written and illustrated several graphic novels. (17)

JOHN RUSH earned a degree in industrial design from the University of Cincinnati. His work can be found in many galleries, including the U.S. Department of the Interior and the French National Government. (18)

BILL WILLIAMS has work displayed in the permanent collections of the National Baseball Hall of Fame, the College Football Hall of Fame, the New York Yankees, and the Butler Institute of American Art. (21)

OWEN SMITH is an illustrator whose work has appeared on the covers of *Rolling Stone*, *Sports Illustrated*, *The New Yorker*, and other magazines, as well as on the walls in the New York City subway system. (22)

JIM SWANSON is an illustrator and fine artist from Wisconsin who was recently named a signature member of the Oil Painters of America. (25)

JULIAN ALLEN The late British artist was a teacher and honored guest of the Smithsonian Institute and The Royal College of Art (London). In 1994 he created a series of stamps depicting famous blues singers for the U.S. Postal Service. (27)

WENDE CAPORALE is a portraitist based in upstate New York; she recently was named a Master Pastelist by the Pastel Society of America. (28)

JULIA LUNDMAN is an art director in San Francisco. She has illustrated work for Disney, Nickelodeon, Random House, and other film and publishing companies. (30)

MARK SAUCK is a Hanover Park, Illinois painter who specializes in outdoor scenery and renditions of dramatic countryside buildings. (33)

JASON MILLET has done illustrations, storyboards, and concept art for advertising, publishing, television, and film. His clients include NBC-Universal, Showtime, Fox, Disney, and Scholastic Books. (35)

BOB CROFUT The New England artist's paintings have appeared in many magazines, including *National Geographic, Time, Smithsonian, Reader's Digest, American Heritage,* and *Yankee.* (36)

NEESA BECKER is an art instructor at the Philadelphia School in Pennsylvania. She is a watercolorist and designer who has illustrated many children's books. (39)

MARY BADENHOP is a Pennsylvania artist whose paintings, which often depict animals, have been used for everything from corporate wall hangings to pillows, pet toys, and greeting cards. (40)

MARK McMAHON The Lake Forest, Illinois painter is from a large family of nationally-known artists. His work, echoing his late father Franklin McMahon's style, adorns the walls of many universities and office buildings. (42)

JEFFREY SMITH is a professor at the Art Center College of Design in Pasadena, California, whose work has won two gold medals from the National Society of Illustrators. (44-45)

LEE MacLEOD is a Santa Fe, New Mexico visual artist whose depictions of desert scenes are nationally recognized, and who has done advertising art for such movies as *Batman* and *Pocahontas.* (47)

JOHN SANDFORD is an author and painter who has done illustrations for over sixty children's books and has won the Parent's Choice Gold Award for his paintings. (48)

JENNIFER KOURY is a Buffalo, New York–based watercolorist whose work has been shown at many galleries and is featured at George Washington's Mount Vernon and the Yuma (Arizona) Regional Medical Center. (51)

ED PASCHKE Paintings by the late Neo-Expressionist are held in many museum collections, including the Art Institute of Chicago, the Whitney Museum in New York, and the Centre Pompidou in Paris. In 2014 the Ed Paschke Art Museum opened in Chicago. (52)

NICK BUBASH is a Pittsburgh-based tattoo artist, who worked early on with Peter Max and Thom DeVita, before graduating with highest honors from the Pennsylvania Academy of the Fine Arts in Philadelphia. (55)

FRANKLIN McMAHON The late "artist-reporter" was a renowned craftsman who created on-the-scene paintings of dramatic moments from the late twentieth century, including civil rights trials and spacecraft launchings. (56)

KEN CALL studied in Paris and at the American Academy of Art and has won many awards for his paintings. He is a Master Signature member of the Transparent Watercolor Society of America. (59)

TIM ANDERSON is a portraitist and image painter whose work can be found in collections around the world, including in the U.S. embassies in Moscow, Bosnia and Herzegovina, and Zimbabwe. (60)

MOSES X. BALL A self-described "people painter," Ball is a Los Angeles–based professional muralist whose work on city walls in Illinois and California have inspired citizens with their civic-minded themes. (63)

LOUISE BEAL (NEE' **POPOFF)** is a watercolor and colored pencil artist based in the Smoky Mountains of North Carolina. Beal created the covers and designs for the beloved Chinaberry Books catalogues for nearly two decades, earning fans worldwide for her whimsical creations. (64)

JÖZEF SUMICHRAST Born in Indiana, the modernist painter and sculptor has had work exhibited from France to Japan and has won awards in countries as diverse as Brazil, Czechoslovakia, Finland, and Cyprus. (66)

RICHARD FORSTER A native of southern Illinois, Forster spent a number of years in Key West, Florida documenting local color, particularly the island's animals and butterflies. (68)

TONY FITZPATRICK is an artist, poet, essayist, and actor whose collages and paintings adorn numerous album covers and posters and hang in the Art Institute of Chicago and the Museum of Modern Art in New York City. (72)

PEGGY MACNAMARA is the longtime artist-in-residence at the Field Museum of Natural History in Chicago. She has traveled the world with scientists, documenting nature and illustrating conservation projects. (75)

TODD TELANDER Based in Walla Walla, Washington, Telander has illustrated several butterfly, bird, and fish guidebooks and has been an artist-in-residence at Rocky Mountain (Colorado) National Park. He is a (previously unknown) relative of the author. (76)

JEAN KIM is a Korean-American artist based in San Francisco and Seoul, Korea who works in acrylics and ink. She specializes in illustrations for children's books with fanciful themes (79)

SAMANTHA DeCARLO is a versatile fine artist whose work has been shown in many art galleries in the Midwest. DeCarlo most enjoys surprising herself with abstract interpretations of varied themes, often with details from nature. (80)

DOUGLAS KLAUBA studied at the American Academy of Art in Chicago and the Academy of Art College in San Francisco. He has illustrated many books, magazines, and posters. (83)

CHRIS DUNN The revered, much-in-demand British watercolorist has illustrated such classic books as the *Wind in the Willows* and *The Night Before Christmas*. (86)

JOSEPH LORUSSO is a fine artist who earned his B.F.A. from the Kansas City Art Institute. Lorusso's classically-influenced paintings have won many awards and are collected in several art museums. (88–89)

AL BRANDTNER is a Chicago-based artist and designer. He has developed unique type fonts, designed over 700 album covers, and his faux postage stamps were displayed at the Museum of Fine Arts in Budapest, Hungary. He designed this book.

RICK TELANDER is a member of the National Sportswriters Hall of Fame. He wrote the poems, and these are his artist friends.

*I LOVE THEM ALL!